Supertrucks

Sloan Walker
and
Andrew Vasey

Walker and Company
New York

This book is dedicated to the tables down at Richter's and the Lynwood College Association, who filled them.

First published in the United States of America in 1985 by the Walker Publishing Company, Inc.

Library of Congress Cataloging-in-Publication Data

Walker, Sloan.
  Supertrucks.

  1. Trucks--Popular works.   I. Vasey, Andrew.
II. Title.
TL230.W3 1985   629.2'24   85-5379
ISBN 0-8027-6586-6
      0-8027-6606-4 (reinforced)

Printed in the United States of America

10 9 8 7 6 5 4 3 2 1

Book design by Laurie McBarnette

Introduction

Most of us don't look twice at the trucks we see every day. The average delivery van isn't very exciting. But some trucks perform unusual functions, such as towing a locomotive or moving the Space Shuttle. If these trucks crossed our path, we would certainly take notice. They are the supertrucks.

We often don't see supertrucks because many of them are one-of-a-kind models that were custom built for a specific function. *Supertrucks* brings them out from behind the scenes and applauds the engineers and designers who have created trucks that can handle just about anything. Words that are set in **bold-face** type are defined in the glossary.

Sloan Walker
Andrew Vasey

Oshkosh

Many of the supertrucks in this book were built by a company called Oshkosh in the Wisconsin city of the same name. Almost everybody has heard of General Motors or Ford, but only dedicated supertruck fans know of Oshkosh. When the United States Marines or an international airport need a tailor-made truck for their operations, they call Oshkosh.

FIRE TRUCKS

Super Fire Truck

This supertruck is not just a fire engine; it's also an airport crash truck and a rescue vehicle. That's why it has large tires with deep treads to grab the road and such an oddly shaped cab. The underside of the cab slopes down to enable the truck to travel through shallow streams. The metal arm above the cab is used to pump fire-fighting foam.

This Oshkosh giant is forty-seven feet long and weighs one hundred and thirty thousand pounds. That makes it the world's largest fire truck.

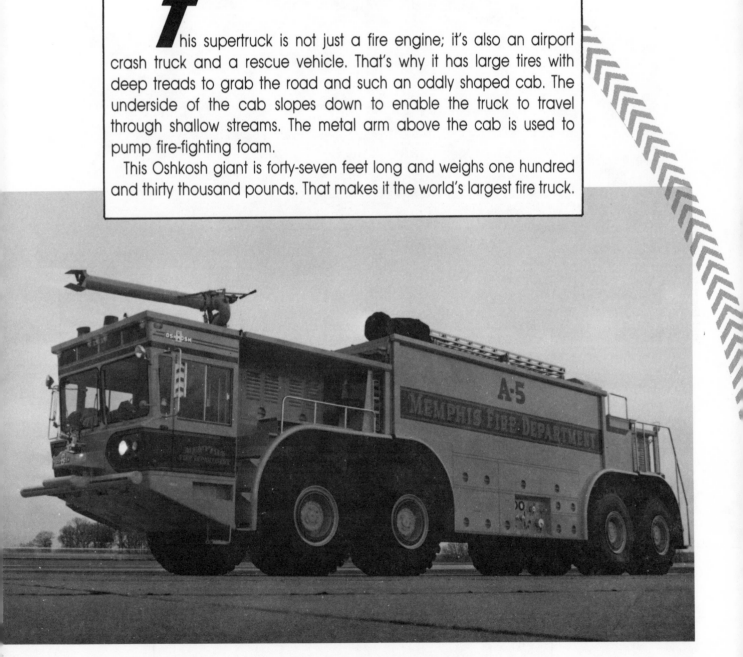

Rock County Fire Truck

Rock County's engine #19 is not quite as huge as the Memphis A-5, but it's not a subcompact, either. This Oshkosh fire truck has **four-wheel drive**, which allows it to go almost anywhere. The midsection is a tank containing densely packed foam.

Like the A-5, engine #19 is used to battle tough fires. It's unlikely that you'll find it responding to every cat-in-the-tree call in the county.

Fire Bug

People have always had a fascination with fire trucks, especially people who design vehicles. A famous designer created this showstopping, fantasy fire truck. The Fire Bug was designed by George Barris, who also built the General Lee, the Knight Rider, and the Batmobile.

This little fire truck is decked out with some fancy equipment, but you would feel more confident fighting fires with one of the heavy-duty Oshkosh trucks.

POLICE VEHICLES

Emergency Police Trucks

Although most people only see patrol cars, police departments also use very special trucks in serious situations. The New York City Police Department uses an Emergency Service Unit to handle its most dangerous problems, such as bombs and riots.

The specially trained police officers in the Emergency Service Unit use three types of trucks. Several of the small trucks are driven out on patrol to back up the regular police officers when they request help. These trucks are equipped with gear for use in disturbances and in rescues. They carry shotguns, portable lights, ladders, an assortment of small tools, and first-aid equipment.

The large Emergency Squad truck (bottom) is called for only when such serious problems as bad road accidents, heavy rescues, and hostage situations arise. It is equipped with ropes, jacks, ladders, and portable air tanks for rescues; and tear gas, shotguns, and bulletproof vests for riots and disturbances. It also has a generator to power lights and other electrical devices.

Bomb Disposal Truck

This larger vehicle with the basket in the rear is the bomb disposal truck. Most police departments use trucks with open tops that will deflect an exploded bomb high up into the air. But this requires open areas where the fragments can scatter without harming people or property. Because New York City is so crowded, the police must have a truck that can withstand an explosion and contain all the fragments.

This bomb disposal truck was built in the 1930s by steelworkers. Only one other truck like this one exists, and it is also owned by the New York City police. The steelworkers wove the basket with steel bridge cables and attached it to a flatbed trailer. The truck has withstood, without any damage, an explosion of eight sticks of dynamite.

*T*he dangerous job of placing the bomb into the truck used to be done by a police officer. In 1983, the New York City Police Department started using a Remote Mobile Investigator (RMI), a robot. The RMI is controlled by a police officer who is a safe one hundred and fifty feet away. The camera on the top of the RMI shows the operator what the arm is picking up. The RMI picks up the bomb and sets it into the sled. The sled then is pulled up the ramp by a cable attached to a winch. The bomb is contained in the truck, and no one gets hurt.

World's Longest Bus

This bus—more than sixty-two feet in length—is the longest bus in the world. The Wayne Corporation in Richmond, Indiana, built it for an oil company in Egypt. Pulled by a diesel-powered truck, the bus can carry up to one hundred and eighty-seven people, more than three times the capacity of an ordinary school bus.

The extra-long bus takes workers to and from the desert oil fields. Fortunately, it doesn't have to go around any sharp curves, because the land in Egypt is very flat and the roads to the oil fields are as straight as arrows.

Prison Bus

The General Motors bus pictured here is owned by the New York City Department of Corrections. This was an ordinary school bus that was modified for the purpose of driving prisoners to and from jail.

The driver is separated from the prisoners by a steel screen. Another screen separates the guard from the prisoners. Heavy steel window screens prevent the prisoners from escaping. A steel door is unlocked only to let the prisoners in and out.

NOVELTY ADVERTISING TRUCKS

Oscar Mayer Wienermobile

The Oscar Mayer Company makes hot dogs and uses the Wienermobile to advertise them. Wienermobiles have been around for about forty years and have gone through some changes over that time. The early models were metal, but now they are made of fiberglass to last longer and use fuel more efficiently.

Channel 2-Mobile

This Channel 2-Mobile, owned by WGBH-TV in Boston, Massachusetts, attracts attention to the public broadcasting station. The body of the 2-Mobile is made of wood, with openings for windows, a door, and access to the engine.

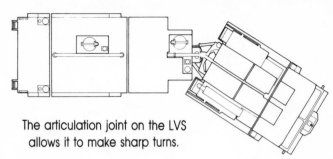

The articulation joint on the LVS allows it to make sharp turns.

The LVS

This oversized dune buggy has a name to match—the Logistical Vehicle System (LVS). Built by Oshkosh, the LVS is an articulated, high **mobility** truck It is called articulated because the front and rear halves are hinged together by an articulation joint. This gives the truck greater mobility on turns than the straight-frame trucks have.

Unlike most articulated **tractor**-trailer trucks—or semis, in truck driver lingo—the LVS has **drive wheels** that supply power to the road in both the trailer and the tractor. In fact, all eight wheels are drive wheels, making the LVS a big jeep.

Although it can't swim, as the photo might suggest, the LVS can cross streams up to five feet deep. And without the cargo box on the trailer, it's not very tall. It can be flown in a United States Air Force transport plane.

Imagine the hit you'd make at the next beach party if you pulled up in this monster jeep!

Air Force Cargo Loader

You wouldn't walk into a General Motors showroom and ask to see the latest model in aircraft loading vehicles. You could, however, talk to Oshkosh about it. Oshkosh built thirty of these cargo loaders for the United States Air Force. Each one can lift forty thousand pounds of cargo to a height of thirteen feet.

To help move heavy cargo once it's on board, three hundred and forty-eight rollers are assembled on the platform. The loader is surprisingly nimble: the platform can tilt forward or backward, left or right. It would make a great ride at an amusement park!

Expanded Mobility Tactical Trucks

Oshkosh builds these eight-wheel-drive trucks for the United States Army. Shown here are the straight-frame cargo truck and the tanker truck.

Unlike articulated trucks, a straight-frame vehicle does not bend in the middle while turning corners. These trucks have replaced the old cargo and troop trucks in use since World War II. They are built to ride high off the ground so they won't get stuck in holes on rocky terrain. The engine powers all eight wheels. If two wheels get stuck, the other six wheels can pull the truck free.

Besides the cargo and tanker trucks, Oshkosh makes a recovery vehicle with a crane, a heavy-duty truck to pull trailers, and a cargo truck with an attached crane to lift supplies in and out of the cargo area.

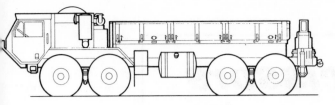

M977—cargo truck with crane

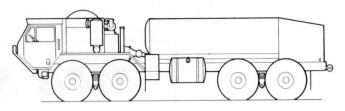

M978—tanker truck

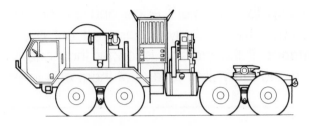

M983—truck tractor with crane

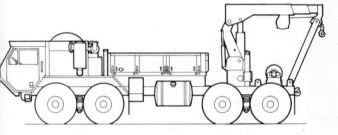

M984—recovery vehicle with crane

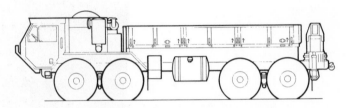

M985—cargo truck with heavy-duty crane

Mobile Assault Bridge

*T*his curious creation is known as a Mobile Assault Bridge (MAB). The Army uses it to raft trucks across streams and shallow rivers.

The MAB also can construct instant bridges. The platforms on the rear of the truck unfold and—in a snap—the soldiers have a way to cross a small ravine.

MAB Scissors

Here's a mobile bridge in action. The MAB drives up to the water's edge and unloads its folding roadway. The roadway is scissored out over floating **pontoons**. If the crossing is longer than one MAB can reach, the Army uses several of them end to end.

Mobile Bridge Launchers

The Army uses bridge launchers to cross a wide valley. Each mobile bridge launches its platforms out in front and drops a support arm to the ground. Then the next bridge launcher drives up the platform and does the same. In this way, the Army can create a bridge as long as it needs—anywhere. Pretty ingenious!

Here's a brain teaser: How do you think the bridge launchers get across?

Ferry

Even though MABs are **amphibious,** they can't cross very deep rivers, so the Army uses mini-ferries like this one. It takes lots of trips back and forth to ferry an entire Army division.

NASA VEHICLES

NASA
Crawler-Transporter

The National Aeronautics and Space Administration (NASA) uses a truck the size of a baseball field to move rockets from the preparation bay to the launch pad. It is called a crawler-transporter, weighs five million pounds, and is self-propelled.

A rocket is loaded onto the huge, flat top and slowly driven to the launch pad. There it is lifted off the transporter and attached to an arming tower.

Because it's so large, the vehicle's top speed is only about one mile an hour. To get an idea of just how big it is, look at the lower right-hand corner of the photograph showing the transporter moving the Space Shuttle. See the man standing next to the fire truck?

The Moonscope

Although it was never used on the moon, George Barris's Moonscope would have been a great ride for the astronauts. It has six-wheel drive and oversized truck tires for driving in and out of craters. Its independent suspension would smooth out the bumps over the moon rocks.

With three television cameras mounted on the front, rear, and top, the astronauts could see everything around them by scanning the three TV screens on the dashboard. The antennas on the hood would allow the astronauts to be in constant contact with their spaceship.

MUNICIPAL TRUCKS

Super Snowblower

If you have a snowblower to clear your driveway, you know how powerful these little machines are. By comparison, this snowblower is a superpower. The Oshkosh H is a high-speed blower used by airports.

The truck can blow away an amazing fifty tons of snow a minute! It clears runways quickly, even in major snowstorms.

Heavy=duty Garbage Truck

This odd-looking contraption is International Harvester's efficient new **diesel** truck. A large mechanical arm on the truck clamps onto a garbage dumpster. The driver pushes a button and the arm raises up, tossing the garbage from the dumpster into the back of the truck. Then the arm lowers the dumpster to the ground—and the driver never has to leave his cab.

Airport Snowplow

This Oshkosh P truck may look a little funny because of its small body and big plow. But any airport would be happy to have it around when a blizzard hits. It has four-wheel drive for excellent **traction** and enough lights to make you think a UFO has landed.

A second, smaller plow in front of the rear wheels provides a close shave. The rear section also carries sand that is sprinkled on the runways for traction after the blades have done their job.

Telephone Pole Truck

Notice that the tires of this truck are not touching the ground. The truck rests on four supports: two come straight down behind the front wheels, and two stretch out in back. These supports keep the truck level, which it has to be to raise and secure power-line towers. A tilt in the truck would cause a leaning tower.

The license plates reveal that this Oshkosh F truck works in Nevada, where it gets pretty hot. The ingenious workmen attached two water coolers to the front bumper. They bolted a water dispenser on the edge of the bumper. When the men get overheated, a splash and a cold drink are always nearby.

Tower Truck

This Oshkosh L vehicle looks like a ladder truck for a fire company. Actually, it is used to maintain electrical lines that run high above the street.

The tower can reach one hundred feet in the air when fully extended—as high as a ten-story building. Because nobody wants to wobble when they're that high up, four support arms keep the truck stable.

The **cab** is extra low to enable the truck to get through tunnels and under bridges.

FUTURE TRUCKS

VEEV Truck
The Veev Future

The basic shape of tractor-trailer trucks hasn't changed much over the past twenty years. But concern about the high cost of fuel may soon bring some changes. International Harvester Company is testing a truck called the VEEV, which stands for Very Energy-Efficient Vehicle. It is designed to be much more **aerodynamic** and fuel-efficient than the trucks of today.

The rounded front and smooth sides allow the truck to slip easily through the air at high speeds. The high cab gives drivers more sleeping space than they have now.

These photos show the VEEV in its early design stage along with a working model to test the aerodynamics under actual driving conditions.

CONSTRUCTION TRUCKS

CAT 777 Dump Truck

*T*he Caterpillar Company builds some of the most powerful construction equipment in the world. The machines on these pages do the backbreaking work that at one time was done by men using carts and shovels. These trucks are used to build highways, create reservoirs, and dig foundations for skyscrapers.

The dump truck shown here is the CAT 777, weighing in at eighty-five tons! That makes it the world's largest dump truck. It's so big, in fact, that it can't be driven on public streets—it's too wide, too tall, too heavy. But on a construction site, this supertruck fits right in.

Payloader

*T*he tractor loading the CAT is called an articulated wheeled **payloader** The articulation hinge on this payloader is behind the front tires. The design allows it to turn much more sharply than an ordinary payloader can.

Bulldozer

The king of this mountain is a CAT D10 track-type bulldozer. It weighs 114,653 pounds—a small mountain in itself. The hook-shaped equipment in the rear is a **hydraulic** ripper to loosen rocks.

A track-type machine like this one has an interesting way of turning. To turn left, the driver stops the left track, and the right track pushes the tractor around to the left. In other words, the tractor pivots on the unmoving track.

The D10's engine puts out over seven hundred **horsepower**. This is one cat that roars!

Cement Mixer

Here's a beautiful, highly efficient cement mixer, called a forward placement mixer. It has the cement chute up front, unlike most cement mixers. The driver can operate the truck and the chute at the same time, to place the cement exactly where it's needed.

The engine is in the rear, behind the mixer. Notice the huge exhaust stack—nearly as tall as a factory smokestack.

Although you may never have thought of a van as a truck, the van evolved from the old delivery truck. Some people have turned their vans into homes on wheels, with furnished rooms, televisions, telephones, stereos, and wall-to-wall carpeting.

Fixing up a van has some advantages over buying a ready-made camper. You can decorate the outside with your own choice of murals and designs, and you can put anything you like inside. Since the mechanics of a van are nearly the same as a car, the engine can be supercharged and customized easily.

The Super Van

The Super Van and the Starship One are good examples of customized vans. They were both created in the 1970s, when van customizing was at its peak.

The Super Van was designed and built by George Barris, builder of the Fire Bug. He created this van for a movie and gave it some unusual features. The television, stereo, and other electrical equipment run on solar energy. The panels with the circles are solar collectors. They catch the sun's rays and convert them into energy, which is stored in batteries. The interior of the Super Van is fully carpeted and furnished as a living room.

The Starship One

The Starship One is a van that was totally rebuilt. The original Chevy van was cut in half horizontally, and a new windshield, roof, and **spoiler** were added. The front doors were permanently welded to the body, and a gull-wing door on the side was installed. It was also cut in half vertically and lengthened twenty-five inches.

The van's body was remade in steel instead of fiberglass for the sake of durability. It was covered with forty layers or orange and blue paint and murals depicting scenes from *Star Wars*. The Starship One is valued at over $75,000.

SALVAGE TRUCKS

Paystar Oil Field Tandem

This International Harvester truck was custom-built for the Dale Meyer Trucking Company in Odessa, Texas. Since oil wells often are miles from the nearest road, a truck that can haul heavy drilling rigs and pumps over rugged terrain is needed.

The Paystar is about thirty-five feet long and has dual axles at both ends to distribute the weight of its load evenly. Both sets of front wheels can be steered to drive the truck easily over rough ground.

With its three hundred and fifty horsepower engine and a main and auxiliary transmission, the Paystar is well-equipped for its job. Such power is essential to transport oil rigs that weigh up to one hundred thousand pounds. How many tons is that?

Super Tow Truck

If your family car breaks down, you can call the nearest garage to have it towed. But suppose you're the pilot of a 747, and it breaks down on the runway? The answer is simple: You call out this powerful winch-on-wheels.

The winch is the circular equipment in the front that works like a gigantic fishing reel. It holds a coiled steel chain that can be hooked onto the disabled plane. The winch reels the line in, and the truck tows the plane away.

When this supertruck is not handling emergencies, it serves an airport the way a tugboat serves a harbor. It can move planes on the ground more efficiently than the planes can move themselves.

Heavy Hauler

If there are hot rods in the trucking world, this Oshkosh K tractor is certainly one of them. The enormous engine in this supertruck produces six hundred horsepower—more than twice the output of most truck engines.

Its six-wheel drive provides excellent traction. The traction, combined with the powerful engine, make this truck a superior hauler for heavy-duty jobs. Paper companies use it to pull trailers loaded with lumber over the rough dirt roads of their forests.

Glossary

Aerodynamics: The effect of air on a moving vehicle.

Amphibious: The ability to move on both land and water.

Cab: The driver's area of a truck. In big trucks it often includes a bed, so one driver can rest while the other drives.

Diesel: A vehicle powered by an engine that runs on air-compressed fuel.

Drive Wheel: A wheel powered by the engine to push or pull a vehicle.

Four-Wheel Drive: The mechanism that powers all four wheels of a vehicle. In a jeep, all the wheels are drive wheels.

Horsepower: The measure of an engine's energy output

Hydraulic: Powered by water pressure.

Mobility: A vehicle's ability to move and turn easily.

Payloader: A tractor that scoops and loads materials in to dump trucks.

Pontoons: Floating structures used to support a tempo rary bridge.

Spoiler: A dam at the front of a vehicle to prevent air from passing underneath and lifting it up at high speeds Most racing cars have spoilers.

Traction: A vehicle's grip on the road.

Tractor: The front half of an articulated truck, which includes the cab and the engine.

Acknowledgments

Oshkosh Corporation
Caterpillar Tractor Corporation
George Barris Kustom Kars
Vance Corporation
City of New York Police Department
Harry Willet
International Harvester
WGBH-TV Boston
Oscar Mayer and Company
British Telecom
City of New York Department of Corrections
Wayne Corporation
NASA
United States Army